A Horse Named Jack

Written by **Linda Vander Heyden** and illustrated by **Petra Brown**

When Jack greets children on the farm,
he's friendly, frisky—full of charm.

Today, no kids have come to play.
Poor Jack's been stuck inside all day.

He's feeling restless and ignored.

He can't help being…bored, bored—

BORED!

So Jack performs his favorite trick—
he lifts his latch with **one** soft **click**.

Two hinges **creeeak**. Jack loves that sound!
He **clip-clops** out to look around.

Three roosters **cock-a-doodle-doo**.
Jack whinnies out a greeting too.

He shakes **four** grain sacks. **Rrrrrip!** They tear—
and oats go flying everywhere!

Five kittens snoozing in the sun.
Jack licks their fur—away they run!

Six bales of hay, so green and sweet,
just waiting there for Jack to eat.

He watches **seven** spiders spin—

Ewww...something sticky on his chin!

Jack flings his head. His eyes grow wide... as **eight** small piglets **squeal** and hide.

He spies **nine** apples on the shelf.

Jack **reeeeeeeaches** in and helps himself.

Ten fuzzy ducklings flap and splash.

Jack wades in—and out they dash!

Jack sniffs the air.
At last he's **free!**
Yum! What's that smell?
He'll go and see.

Look how nice this garden grows.

Tasty carrots—**rows and rows!**

Why, there's his neighbor! See her run?
Perhaps she's come to join the **fun!**

But what are all those angry shouts?
And what's she so upset about?

She's throwing down the garden hoe!

It's time for Jack to…

go, Go, GO!

Ten tomatoes whizzing past—

that neighbor lady's really fast!

Juicy cherries fall like rain— **nine KERSPLAAAT** in Jack's long mane!

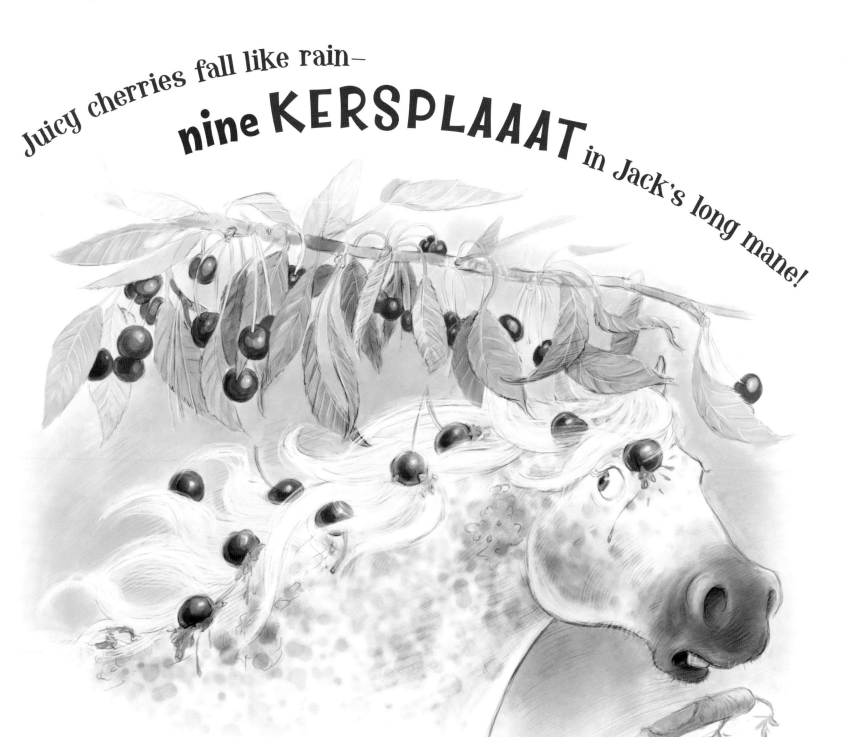

He'll have to hurry—have to race,
for now **eight** dogs have joined the chase!

Seven cats,

six songbirds, too—

five squawking chickens—coming through!

Four bumblebees buzz by his ear.

At last—**Hooray!**—the barn is near!

Jack leaps across **three** hollow logs.

He gallops past **two** bug-eyed frogs.

One muddy puddle lies ahead...
Jack tries to jump—but trips instead!

He's slipping, sliding down the trail— caked with mud from head to tail!

Through the barnyard gate he skids...
Jack's home at last.

"Oh, Jack." They laugh and pet his nose.
"Before we play…

we'll need the hose!"

For Mom and Dad and Korey, with love

—Linda

For my Iain

—Petra

Text Copyright © 2018 Linda Vander Heyden
Illustration Copyright © 2018 Petra Brown
Design Copyright © 2018 Sleeping Bear Press

Sleeping Bear Press®
2395 South Huron Parkway, Suite 200
Ann Arbor, MI 48104
www.sleepingbearpress.com

Printed and bound in the United States.

10 9 8 7 6 5 4 3 2 1

Library of Congress Cataloging-in-Publication Data

Names: Vander Heyden, Linda, author. | Brown, Petra, illustrator.
Title: A horse named Jack / written by Linda Vander Heyden ; illustrated by
Petra Brown.
Description: Ann Arbor, MI : Sleeping Bear Press, [2018] | Summary: Follows a
mischievous horse from one click of the latch on his stall to ten tomatoes
a neighbor throws after he raids her garden and back down to one muddy puddle.
Identifiers: LCCN 2017029872 | ISBN 9781585363957
Subjects: | CYAC: Stories in rhyme. | Horses—Fiction. | Behavior—Fiction. |
Farm life—Fiction. | Domestic animals—Fiction. | Counting.
Classification: LCC PZ8.3.V332 Hor 2018 | DDC [E]—dc23
LC record available at https://lccn.loc.gov/2017029872